DEBBIE BOON

Gio's PIZZAS

MACDONALD YOUNG BOOKS

Signor Gio Fabrizza
Is the very finest cook
His recipes are famous
And that's why he's in this book.

GIO'S PIZZAS

When picking wild mushrooms always consult a reference book.
The mushrooms illustrated in this book are an edible variety known as
Caesar's Mushrooms found amongst woodland in warmer climates.

Text and illustrations copyright © Debbie Boon 1998

First published in Great Britain in 1998
by Macdonald Young Books,
an imprint of Wayland Publishers Ltd
61 Western Road
Hove
East Sussex
BN3 1JD

Find Macdonald Young Books on the internet at
http://www.myb.co.uk

Printed and bound in Portugal by Edições ASA.

British Library Cataloguing in Publication Data available.

ISBN: 0 07500 2503 4

His pizzas are fantastic
There's none that can compare
If you have the luck to try one
You'll never want to share!

His wife is Rose Maria
The expert with the dough
She mixes, kneads and tosses
Oh, the pizzas she can throw!

She spins them to the ceiling
The dough gets even thinner
Then Gio adds his toppings
Each pizza is a winner!

A chef with such a talent
His singing draws a crowd
His solos are quite lovely
The notes are long and loud.

When chopping up the onions
A tear or two he'll cry
But his operatic singing
Helps him peel and slice and fry.

When Gio makes spaghetti
He doesn't use a bowl
He mixes with his fingers
Before it's time to roll.

To make his pasta nice and neat
He needs a rolling pin
He presses very firmly
So that it's nice and thin.

His mamma grows tomatoes
Sun-ripened for the sauce
Her recipe's a secret
But Gio knows, of course.

She loves to sit and smell
The sweet scent of the vines
She rocks gently in her chair
And dreams of olden times.

When Gio wants salami
He knows just where to go
To Luigi's sausage deli
Where everything's on show.

Hanging from the ceiling
There's such a lot to see
Spicy, smoky, take your pick
And choose from twenty-three!

If you visit cousin Bella
Be sure to bring some bread
Try her stretchy mozzarella
"Sensational!" it's said.

The nicest cheese you'll ever try
On a tasty pizza sliced
Or if you're feeling healthy
In a salad diced.

Gio's papa, Carlo
Has a very special hound
He's always right behind him
When there's mushrooms to be found.

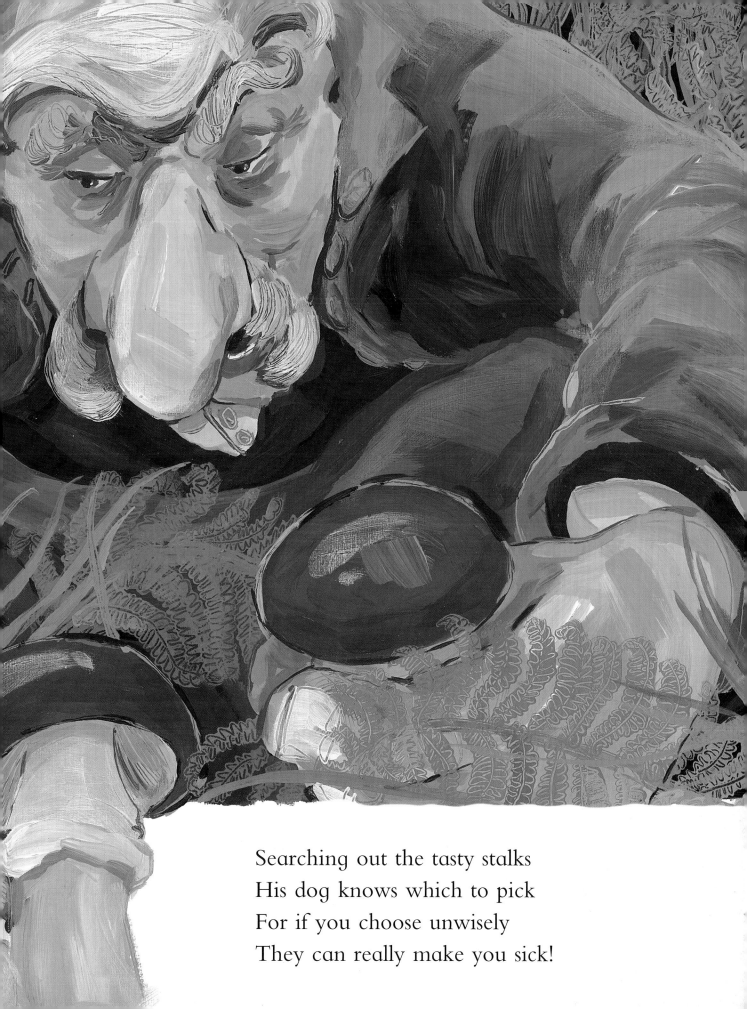

Searching out the tasty stalks
His dog knows which to pick
For if you choose unwisely
They can really make you sick!

When Gio wants to travel
He hates to use the car
Zipping among the traffic
His bike is best by far!

Rose Maria rides behind
Her goggles flashing brightly
She smiles and waves at passers-by
While hugging Gio tightly.

When strolling through the crowded town
That's full of busy feet
If you catch the sound of music
Be sure to take a seat.

It's Gio's brother, Tony
He runs the music bar
His tunes are loud and jazzy
He's really quite a star.

Renato makes the ice cream
His flavours can't be beaten
From Vanilla Peach to Pecan Pie
How many have *you* eaten?

His stall is in the market place
Where he sings about his prices
People come from near and far
To taste his famous ices.

Now Bruno Fontarelli
It simply must be known
Grows the greenest olives
From Parma down to Rome.

To sample Bruno's olive oil
So full of fruity flavours
Is Gio's favourite little treat
Each golden drop he savours!

But when the day is over
And Gio's work is done
It's time to join his family
And really have some fun.

It's been a busy day
And now it's time to rest
For everybody know that
Gio's cooking is the best!

PIZZA BASE

450g (1lb) plain flour
6g sachet dried yeast
1 tsp salt
about 300ml (½ pint)
  hand hot water
olive oil

Sift flour and salt into bowl and add yeast. Mix together. Add warm water bit by bit. Knead until soft and springy.

Cover and leave to rise in warm place. When dough has doubled in size, knead again and divide into 4 balls for individual pizzas.

Roll or press dough into thin circles. Place on an oiled baking sheet. Drizzle with a little olive oil.

Now for the toppings!

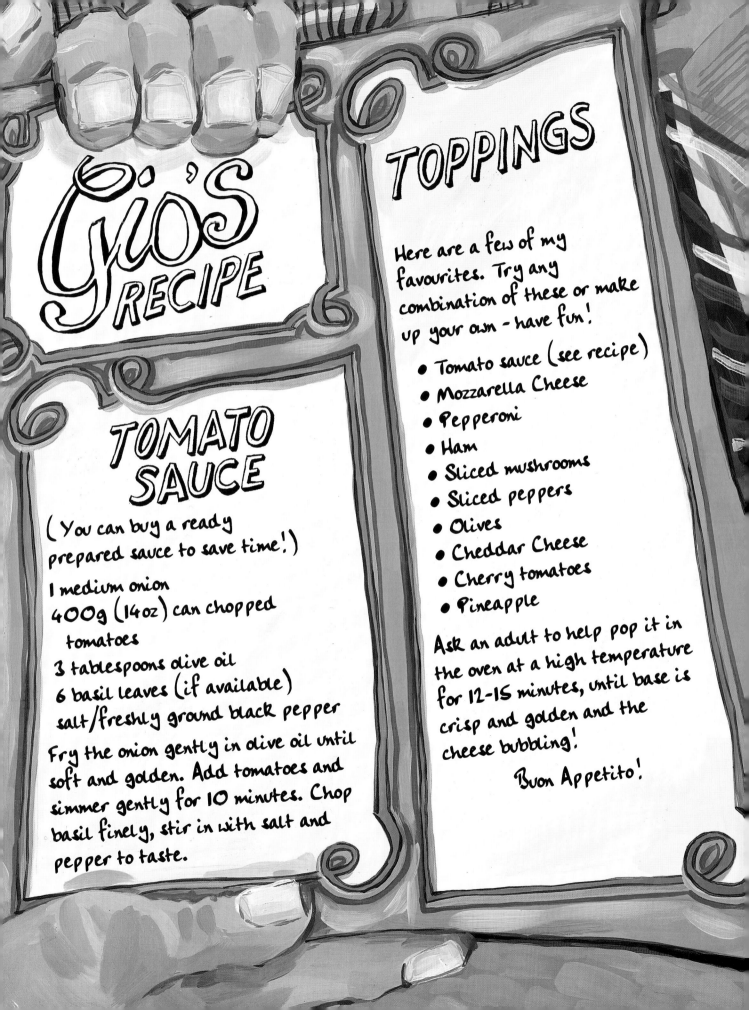

Gio's Recipe

TOMATO SAUCE

(You can buy a ready prepared sauce to save time!)

1 medium onion
400g (14oz) can chopped
   tomatoes
3 tablespoons olive oil
6 basil leaves (if available)
salt/freshly ground black pepper

Fry the onion gently in olive oil until soft and golden. Add tomatoes and simmer gently for 10 minutes. Chop basil finely, stir in with salt and pepper to taste.

TOPPINGS

Here are a few of my favourites. Try any combination of these or make up your own - have fun!

- Tomato sauce (see recipe)
- Mozzarella Cheese
- Pepperoni
- Ham
- Sliced mushrooms
- Sliced peppers
- Olives
- Cheddar Cheese
- Cherry tomatoes
- Pineapple

Ask an adult to help pop it in the oven at a high temperature for 12-15 minutes, until base is crisp and golden and the cheese bubbling!

Buon Appetito!